STAR WARS ™

FINN AND POE TEAM UP!

WRITTEN BY NATE MILLICI

ART BY ANDREA PARISI & GRZEGORZ KRYSINSKI

DISNEP

LUCASFILM
PRESS

Los Angeles • New York

D0888188

Printed in China

First Boxed Set Edition, October 2016   10 9 8 7

Library of Congress Control Number on file

FAC-025393-22178

ISBN 978-1-4847-9040-3

Visit the official *Star Wars* website at: www.starwars.com.

Poe was a pilot.
He fought against
the evil First Order.

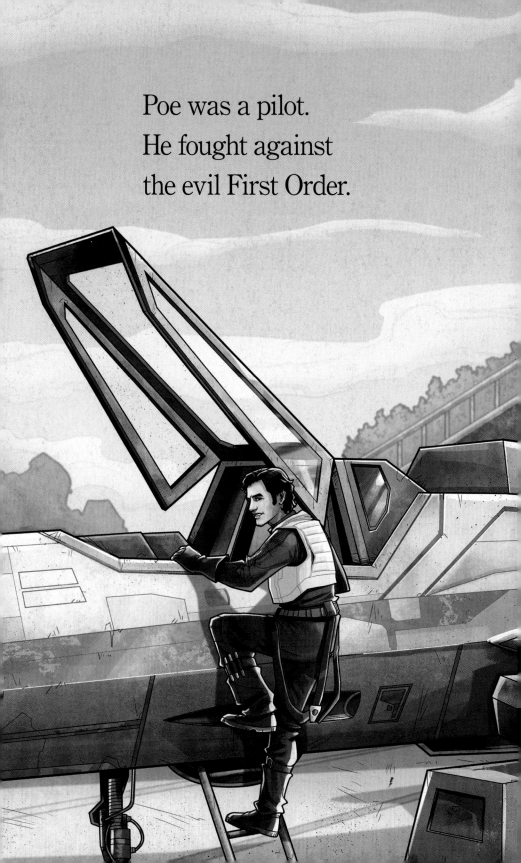

One day, Leia gave Poe
a special mission.

Poe and his droid, BB-8, needed to
find a man named Lor San Tekka.

The First Order wanted
to find Lor San Tekka, too.
But one stormtrooper did not
want to go on the mission.
His name was FN-2187.

Lor San Tekka lived on
a planet called Jakku.
Poe and BB-8 flew to Jakku.
The First Order ships
also flew to Jakku.

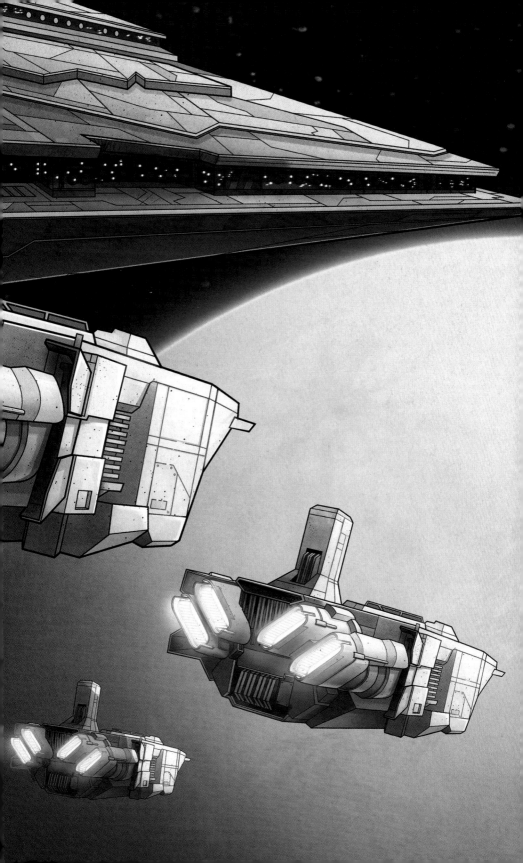

Poe found Lor San Tekka first.
Lor San Tekka gave Poe a map.
The map would help Leia
find her brother, Luke.

Luke was a great Jedi Knight.
Leia thought that Luke could help
stop the First Order.

The First Order troopers
landed on Jakku.

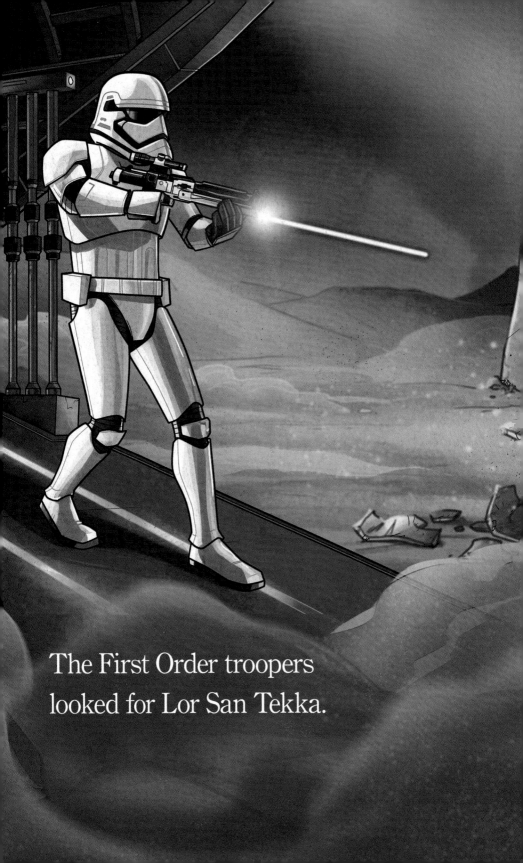

The First Order troopers
looked for Lor San Tekka.

Poe told Lor to hide.
Poe gave the map to BB-8.
Poe did not want the
First Order to find the map.

FN-2187 did not want to
hurt the people on Jakku.
FN-2187 did not want to hurt anyone.

The troopers captured Poe.
They took Poe to Kylo Ren.

Kylo Ren wanted the map.
Kylo Ren was angry when
Poe did not have the map.

The First Order troopers took
Poe back to their ship.
Poe was locked in a prison cell.

Captain Phasma was mad at FN-2187.

Kylo Ren made Poe tell him where the map was hidden. Poe told Kylo Ren that BB-8 had the map.

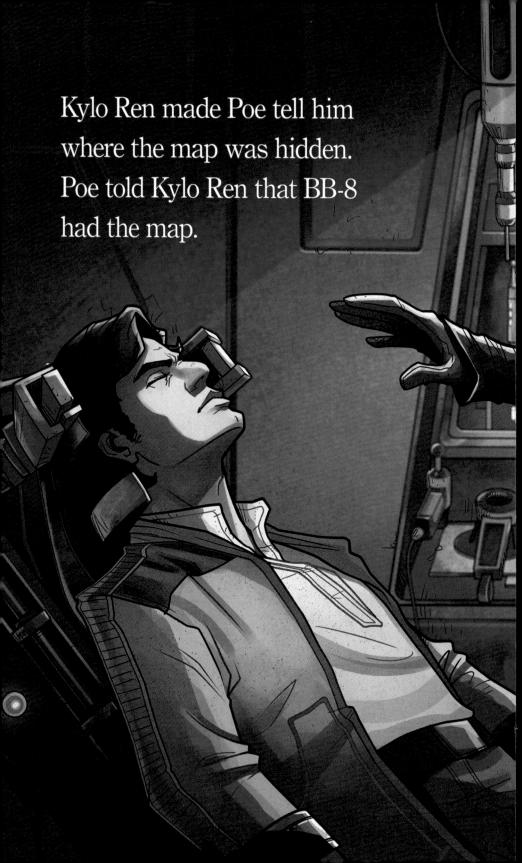

FN-2187 did not want
to be a part of the First Order.
But FN-2187 needed help.

FN-2187 freed Poe.
They would escape
the First Order as a team!

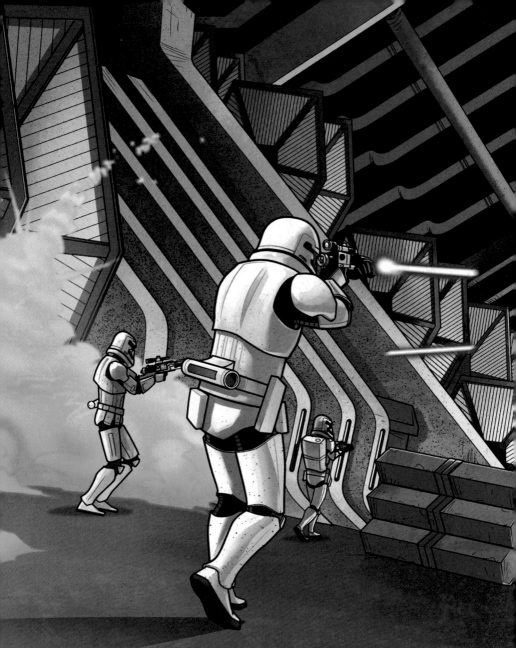

FN-2187 and Poe stole a TIE fighter.
But the troopers put up a fight!

FN-2187 and Poe flew into space.
The First Order ship fired
on their TIE fighter!

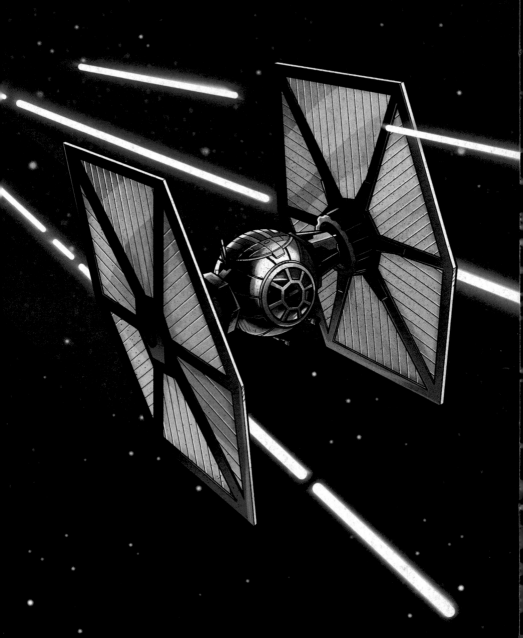

Poe flew the TIE fighter.

FN-2187 fired back at the big ship.

FN-2187 and Poe escaped
from the First Order ship.

Poe was proud of his new friend.
Poe called him Finn.

Poe flew the TIE fighter toward Jakku.
He needed to find BB-8.

Finn and Poe made a great team!